Published by Puffin 2013
A Penguin Company
Penguin Books Ltd, 80 Strand, London, WC2R 0RL, UK
Penguin Group (USA) Inc., 375 Hudson Street, New York 10014, USA
Penguin Books Australia Ltd, 707 Collins Street, Melbourne, Victoria 3008,
Australia (A division of Pearson Australia Group Pty Ltd)
Canada, India, New Zealand, South Africa

Written by Barry Hutchison

www.puffinbooks.com

ISBN: 978-1-40939-295-0
001
Printed in Great Britain

MIX
Paper from
responsible sources
FSC™ C018179
FSC
www.fsc.org

PICK YOUR
PORTAL

THE TROUBLE
WITH DOUBLES

PUFFIN

Today is the rarest of rare things – a trouble-free day in Skylands. The Chompies aren't chomping, the Spider Swarmers aren't swarming, and the Squidface Brutes aren't . . . doing whatever it is Squidface Brutes usually do. Something nasty, no doubt.

Cali has asked a few of the Skylanders to do some training at the ruins, and when Cali asks you to do something, you do it. Unless you're Flynn, in which case you just stand around grinning. Then again, that's all Flynn does most of the time, anyway.

Some of the greatest Skylanders in history have gathered together. Spyro is enjoying the sunshine. Pop Fizz is brewing up a new potion. Fright Rider and Terrafin are sharing battle stories, and Hot Dog is chasing a screaming T-Bone up and down the beach. Stealth Elf is around here somewhere too, but then she's never an easy one to spot.

And then there's you, Portal Master, watching over events from afar, but a vital part of the team all the same. After all, without a Portal Master to help guide them, the Skylanders wouldn't be the legends they are.

A dark shadow suddenly passes across the Skylanders. You all look up to see Flynn's balloon come swooping in from above. As it nears the ground, Cali jumps down, landing expertly on the soft grass.

"Hey, guys, thanks for coming," she says. Behind her, the balloon hits the ground with a *crash*.

"Not a problem," calls a familiar voice from inside the basket. "I absolutely meant to do that."

Flynn stands up and clambers out from within the basket. He rushes over to stand by Cali's side and – yep – there's that grin again.

"As I was saying," Cali continues, "I really appreciate you guys turning up for training. Things have been quiet around here lately, but I have a feeling trouble may be just round the corner, and we need to be ready."

Spyro and the other Skylanders gather round Cali. Even Stealth Elf appears, as if from thin air. They all love rest and relaxation, but they know that the safety of Skylands is more important. If trouble really is coming, then they want to be as prepared as possible to face it.

"I've come up with a great new Heroic Challenge," Cali explains, "designed just for you Skylanders." A frown briefly interrupts the grin on Flynn's face.

"What about me? Don't I get a challenge? I could totally do any challenge you set me."

Cali thinks for a moment. "Good idea. I challenge you to stay quiet for the next ten minutes."

"Too easy," says Flynn.

Cali smirks. "Challenge failed."

The air round the Skylanders begins to flicker and a floating face appears. Everyone recognizes the face at once, and from the expression it wears they know something is wrong.

"Master Eon," says Terrafin. "What's happened?"

"We may have a problem, Skylanders. I've heard rumour of an attack on the Mabu town on Shattered Island."

"An attack?" asks Spyro. "By who?"

"By you, Spyro," says Master Eon gravely. "The reports say that you attacked the town."

The other Skylanders all turn to look at the magical dragon. "Hey, it couldn't have been me, I've been here the whole time!"

"He's right," says Stealth Elf. "Besides, he's Spyro. He's a Skylander. Skylanders don't do things like that."

"Exactly," says Master Eon. "We know it couldn't possibly have been Spyro. So who was it? You must go to the town and see what you can find out."

"Hey, but what about training?" says Cali. "If you guys go rushing in you might find something you can't deal with. Train first, then you'll be better prepared to face whatever's out there."

"Cali's right," agrees Flynn. "But then, Cali's always right. And her hair smells like freshly cut flowers."

"Let's get out there and bust some heads!" says Terrafin.

"It's all just a rumour. We don't even know if anything has happened," says Stealth Elf. "I'm with Cali. We should train first, then go check it out."

"Wheeeee!" says Pop Fizz, pouring a jug of potion over his head. There is a faint *bloop* and his nose turns an unusual shade of purple.

If you think the Skylanders should rush to investigate the attack
, **turn to page 63.**

If you think they should get in some training first, **turn to page 28.**

You decide it's a good idea to stop off with Persephone to see what she can offer. As usual, the fairy is in a bright mood. Unfortunately, her grasp of English hasn't really improved much.

"Skylanders are back! Happy times!"

The Skylanders all greet Persephone and tell her about the attack on the Mabu village.

"Oh, a terrible thing," she gasps. "I can happy dance gold into great power, for helping you on this day. You have gold, yes?"

Pop Fizz rummages in his pockets and produces a bundle of shiny objects. The other Skylanders stare at the bundle for a long, long time.

"Those are teeth," says Terrafin at last. "Why d'you have a pocket full of teeth?"

Pop Fizz glances at the others, then slowly slips the teeth back into his pocket. "Out of gold," he says, and the others all seem to be short of coins too.

"Here, this one's on me," says Flynn, stepping forward. He opens his wallet and some moths fly out. Instead of money there is a note in the wallet. "I owe you," he reads. "Signed, Flynn. Hey, that's me!"

"Oh, out of the way," Cali sighs. She passes Persephone a bag of gold coins.

"Happy gold for a happy dance!" the fairy sings. She

begins to sail and twist in the air, and as she does so the Skylanders begin to feel their strength grow.

"Wow, check this out," says Spyro. He opens his mouth and a vast plume of flame erupts from his throat. It rises like a fiery cloud above the Ruins, making the other Skylanders *oooh* in surprise. Even Terrafin looks impressed, and that doesn't happen very often.

"Not bad, kid," he says. "Not bad at all."

The rest of the team take a few moments to test out their increased abilities, but then it's time to get serious. They thank Persephone for her help, **then head quickly to page 54.**

You send the Skylanders to Falling Forest. Spyro's evil double has got to pay for what it has done to the Mabu town.

As soon as the team arrive, they spot Kaos' minion. For Spyro it's like looking in a mirror – the minion looks exactly like him. Well, maybe a bit darker in places. And its eyes are glowing a funny colour. And its face is all twisted up and wicked. But apart from all that they're identical.

The dragon minion takes to the air as soon as it spots the Skylanders. With a beat of its scaly wings it lifts off, banking upwards over the treetops, and up the steep hill of the Falling Forest.

Spyro isn't about to let him get away that easily. He zooms off in hot pursuit, swooping and slicing through the sky. He quickly notices there's another difference between him and his evil minion – he's much faster!

In no time at all, Spyro begins to close in on the evil double. He's about to make a grab for him when he realizes too late that it's a trick! The dragon minion spins on to his back and lets rip with a magical fireball. It catches Spyro by surprise. Blinded, he plunges down towards the ground.

A clump of trees breaks his fall. His vision clears just in time to see the evil double rocketing at him, claws outstretched.

Spyro twists in the branches and the dragon minion narrowly misses him. It crashes through the trees and lands with a heavy *bump* on the forest floor. As he tries to jump down after him, Spyro discovers his feet are tangled in twisting lengths of vine. A quick blast of his fire breath takes care of those, and he drops down to earth just as the evil double races off through the trees.

"Run all you like," Spyro calls, as he bounds after the minion. "I'm not going to let you get away!"

They are evenly matched for speed. The minion darts left and right, dodging past trees and leaping over trailing roots. Spyro ducks, weaves and bounds his way up the steep hillside, squeezing through the gaps big enough to fit through, and battering down the ones that aren't.

With a final surge, Spyro explodes into a clearing in the forest. Paths lead off in all directions, but there is no sign of the dragon minion anywhere. Spyro stops and listens, hoping to hear something that will tell him which way to go. But all he can hear is the tweeting of birds and chirping of insects until . . . *There!*

A twig snaps up ahead on the right. Spyro bounds into the forest again and in no time he spots his evil double hiding in a clump of bushes up ahead. The minion doesn't realize he's been spotted!

A grin spread across Spyro's face. He's going to enjoy this!

Quick, **hurry to page 70** to discover what Spyro's going to enjoy.

As the walls of the tunnel shake, they seem to close in around the Skylanders. With his arms pinned to his sides, it isn't easy for Pop Fizz to reach a potion bottle. He strains his shoulders, ignoring the pain as he stretches an arm up his back.

"A-a-almost there," he grunts. With a final heave, Pop Fizz manages to grab the neck of the bottle. "I got it!" he cries, and then the bottle slips from his grasp, landing between his feet. "Whoops. I don't got it."

Wiggling himself forward, Terrafin snags the bottle neck between two of his huge toes. With his other foot he grabs hold of the cork and yanks it free with a *plonk*.

"Hurry!" yelps Spyro. The Evil Chop Chop is still watching them through the narrow gap.

"Three, t-two, one – g-go!" says Terrafin, and he brings this foot sharply up so that the bottle curves into the air.

Pop Fizz opens his mouth as wide as he can. The potion drops inside, bottle and all. Then, when he has drained it dry, he spits the empty bottle back out.

There, in the cramped tunnel, Pop Fizz begins to grow and mutate into his beastly berserker form.

The monster's hot breath blasts against the back of Terrafin's head. "Uh . . . this is a good thing, right?" he wonders aloud. "I'm not about to be eaten here, am I? "

Suddenly, the walls squeezing the Skylanders inch

away. Finding themselves with room, they turn and see Pop Fizz growing so much he is forcing the walls apart!

With a savage roar, he presses his hands against the walls and pushes. His powerful muscles strain as he forces them outwards.

With a sharp jerk, Spyro lunges forward, headbutting Evil Chop Chop and slamming him against a jagged outcrop of rock. "Don't get up," Spyro warns. "You *really* don't want to make my big blue friend back there angry."

Wisely, the skeleton minion does as he is told. Behind Pop Fizz, Evil Stealth Elf appears and hurls herself at the berserker's broad back. She is about to slice at him with her blades when the real Stealth Elf flips over Pop Fizz's shoulders and deflects the attack.

Stealth Elf kicks her double in the stomach, before knocking her legs from under her in one sweeping move. One last kick knocks her unconscious.

Pop Fizz finishes pushing the walls apart, and not a moment too soon. Whatever is causing the tremors is bringing the whole corridor down!

They race for the exit, dodging falling rocks. The whole underground is collapsing. Whatever Kaos was up to, it's too late to stop it now. You may have defeated a couple of minions, but their boss has managed to put his plan into action.

Oh dear. Master Eon *will* be disappointed.

THE END

"Time to bring out the big guns," says Terrafin. He swaps his brass knuckles for a set of spiked ones. "I warn you, bucket-head, this is really going to hurt!"

Keeping his chin tucked in to his chest, Terrafin approaches the Arkeyan Hammah.

"Seconds out, round three," announces Pop Fizz.

There is a real tension in the air. Everyone seems to know that this fight is going to be over soon.

BOOM! Terrafin lands an explosive jab on the force field. It ripples like the surface of a lake.

BANG! A right hook staggers the Hammah. The Skylanders cheer and the evil minions look at the exit.

THUD! A left uppercut inflicts more damage on the force field. It crackles, then disappears completely.

MISS! Terrafin swings a double-handed punch. The Hammah leans back and Terrafin stumbles forward.

Before the Skylander can turn, the Hammah's weapon smashes him on the head, slamming him to the floor.

Never one to quit, Terrafin tries to get up, but another Hammah blow knocks his arms out from under him and this time he doesn't get up. Terrafin has been defeated, and with the minions and the Arkeyan robot to deal with, the Skylanders will have a real fight on their hands if they hope to get out of this cavern in one piece.

THE END

Taking your advice, Pop Fizz draws back his hairy arm and launches the potion towards the Arkeyan Hammah. It seems to go into slow motion as it sails through the air.

The Skylanders hold their breaths and follow the bottle's flight.

The minions stare in wonder as the concoction tumbles down, down, down towards the unsuspecting Hammah.

And then the bottle explodes harmlessly against the Hammah's force field, and Pop Fizz can only watch as his precious potion trickles away down the cracks in the hard stone floor.

"Oh man," he sighs, as the last of the liquid seeps through the gaps, "I'm toast."

Pop Fizz barely has time to brace himself before the Hammah's weapon smacks against his head with a hollow *thonk*. The floor suddenly feels soft and spongy beneath the gremlin's feet. The cavern seems to spin around him, and somewhere in the distance he can hear the sound of birds tweeting.

It looks like someone made a bad decision somewhere, Portal Master, and without pointing any fingers or laying any blame, it looks like that someone was *definitely* you.

THE END

You decide to rely on Hot Dog's famous sense of smell.
Fright Rider tries really hard to argue with you, but when
Hot Dog zips off through the door on the right, he has no
choice but to follow along behind the other Skylanders.

Hot Dog darts this way and that, snuffling at the floor,
quickly twisting and turning his way through the dimly-
lit passageways. As he scampers round a sharp bend
he suddenly skids to a complete stop. There, totally
blocking the path, is the biggest Stump Demon the
Skylanders have ever clapped eyes on. Its branches make
a rustling noise as it turns and fixes the heroes with a
wicked glare.

There is a *shnink* sound as Stealth Elf unsheathes her
dragonfang daggers in one quick motion. She is just
about to hurtle herself towards the Stump Demon when
the ground starts to to tremble and shake under her.
A fast-moving shape churns up the rock and soil beneath
her feet as it thunders towards the Stump Demon,
and then . . .

KABOOM!

Terrafin erupts out of the ground and smashes
a particularly powerful fist into the Stump Demon's
startled face, right where its nose would be (if Stump
Demons actually had noses). The tree creature's eyes
cross. Its mouth drops open. Then, with a groaning of

roots and branches, it slowly topples backwards onto the ground.

"Timmmm-beeeeerrrrr!" shouts Terrafin at the top of his voice, just as the Stump Demon hits the floor with an almighty *THUMP*.

Terrafin turns and flexes his impressive muscles but, as he does, another Stump Demon emerges from the shadows, its terrifying jaws snapping hungrily at the musty air.

"Hey," Hot Dog barks at the approaching Stump Demon, grinning a knowing grin. "You'd better back off, branch-for-brains. You do know what dogs do to trees, don't you?"

Slowly, Hot Dog raises his back leg. The Stump Demon's face falls. It gives a slightly embarrassed cough, and then slips back into the shadows once again.

"I don't get it," frowns Pop Fizz. "What do dogs do to trees?"

"Trust me," says Spyro. "You don't want to know."

Hot Dog carries on leading the way through, and soon the Skylanders emerge into the fresh air. Not that the air is ever very fresh in the Darklight Crypt, of course, but you get the idea. Cali is there waiting with Flynn, who is manically waving a small flag and wearing a funny, brightly coloured party hat.

"Woo-hoo! I knew you'd make it," says Flynn. "I never had any doubt."

"Then why did you say you didn't think we'd ever see them again?" asks Cali.

"Oh, just my little joke, Cali."

"You were crying and everything," Cali says.

Flynn waves his flag again, looking distinctly more sheepish this time. "Woo-hoo!"

Cali can't help but smile at the back-tracking Mabu pilot.

You transport everyone back to the Ruins. Hot Dog paces round and round in a circle then lies down, curling up into a ball.

"What are you doing?" asks Spyro. "We need to go investigate those attacks."

Hot Dog yawns. "I just need five minutes to have a little rest. It's extremely tiring work having a nose this awesome."

"We need to go now," urges Stealth Elf.

Terrafin sits down to rest too, with his back against a rock. "The mutt's right. Five minutes won't hurt us. We should all get our breaths back before heading out there."

What do you think, Portal Master? Should they take a few minutes to catch their breaths? **Head over to page 38** if you think so.

Or have they wasted enough time already? **Turn to page 54** if you think they should get to work right away.

Portal Master, Portal Master, Portal Master. Tut, tut, tut.

You decide to send the team to Falling Forest to find the scheming villain behind the attacks, but what about the poor Mabu at the town? It's all very well pummelling bad guys, but innocent lives are at stake here. Don't you know the hero's code? A true hero should always protect the innocent before all else. With the Skylanders off chasing evil minions, who is there to protect the Mabu? No one, that's who.

If you listen carefully, you can almost hear the screams of the Mabu as their town collapses around their ears. Like Gill Grunt's singing, it is a sound that will haunt the Skylanders for the rest of their lives. Oh dear.

THE END

You send the Skylanders after the Terrafin and Gill Grunt doubles. Hot Dog and Fright Rider close in on them as they head through a doorway. The two Skylanders hurtle through into a huge domed chamber, then stop. The other Skylanders arrive to find them gazing up at something above them.

"Is that what I think it is?" whispers Stealth Elf.

"Oh, you bet it is," cackles the Gill Grunt double.

"Bet you wish you hadn't come sticking your nose in," Evil Terrafin grins. "You're in trouble now!"

Hot Dog Firebarks a ball of flame at the minions. Ablaze, they run squealing in circles.

"Now," says Fright Rider. "What do we do about *that*?"

The Skylanders stare up at the towering figure looming over them. Even at this massively increased size, you'd recognize that bald head anywhere.

"Kaos," spits Spyro.

"Greetings, Skylanders," bellows Kaos. "How annoying that you could join us. I had hoped the little stunt with my dragon minion and the Mabu town would have kept you busy, but here you are."

"You know us," shrugs Spyro. "Annoying you is what we live for."

"Well, lucky for me you won't be living for long!" he shrieks. "Glumshanks! Destroy them! BWAH-HA-HA!"

There's a scuffing sound and the head of Kaos' faithful troll butler emerges. Glumshanks stares at the Skylanders, then up at his massive boss.

"Uh . . . me?"

"Yes, you!" yells Kaos. "Must I do everything myself?!"

Glumshanks blinks. "Well . . . I'd prefer if you did. You know, we did go to all that trouble to make you huge. It would seem a bit of a waste not to make use of that."

"Oh very well!" Kaos bellows. "Bring it on, *Cry*-landers!"

Glumshanks ducks back down behind the rock. "I'll be hiding here if you need me."

Your team of heroes is ready. All they need now is for you to decide how best to launch the attack.

And remember, Portal Master, it isn't just the Skylanders at risk here – lose this battle and all of Skylands could fall beneath Kaos' new-found might.

Should you go with Battle Plan A?: All Skylanders race for Kaos' closest foot and try to bring him down that way. If you like the sound of that plan, **turn to page 58**.

Or how about Battle Plan B?: The Skylanders spread out and try attacking him from different angles in the hope of finding a weak spot. If you think this is the way to go, **get yourself over to page 50** right now.

Sometimes a more sneaky approach is called for, and you think now is one of those times. You send Stealth Elf to follow the minions while the other Skylanders hang back, keeping watch for trouble.

Stealth Elf seems to melt away before your very eyes. She moves up the steps like a whisper, getting close enough to the minions to hear what they're saying.

"Those Skylanders are idiots," grunts Evil Gill Grunt. "I bet they're off chasing the Dragon Minion around the Falling Forest."

"Yup, Kaos sure is smart," says Evil Chop Chop. The others look at him in surprise. "Well . . . you know. Sometimes," he adds.

"Oh yeah, *sometimes*," agrees Evil Terrafin. "He's definitely smart *sometimes*."

"Just not that often," concludes Evil Stealth Elf. The real Stealth Elf has to resist the urge to lunge at the impostor with her twin blades. It isn't easy, but she remembers that her mission is to find information – not to fight.

She follows the minions up the steps. They chatter about how stupid the Skylanders are for a while, and about how useless the heroes are when it comes to fighting.

Just wait, Stealth Elf thinks. *We'll see who's useless.*

The steps keep curving up and up, before disappearing into a cave shaped like a dragon's head at the top. The minions scuttle inside and Stealth Elf follows, her ninja skills leading her instinctively into the shadows.

There is a wooden door at the back of the cave. It opens with a *creak* as the evil minions approach and they march through one at a time. Moving quickly, Stealth Elf only just manages to squeeze through before the door slams closed once more.

Beyond the door is a dimly lit hallway, with several more doors leading off in different directions.

"What would you do if a Skylander walked in here right now?" asks the Evil Chop Chop.

"Easy," snorts Evil Terrafin. "I'd pound 'em until they were just a puddle on the floor."

"Ha! No way, I'd harpoon them before you could lift a finger," cackles the minion who looks like Gill Grunt. "They wouldn't stand a chance."

"Fools," snorts the Evil Stealth Elf. "My wicked stealth makes me faster than any of you. I'd have them all tied up and fed to a troll before you lot had even noticed they'd arrived." Her eyes gleam with excitement. "Especially Stealth Elf. I'd show her how a *real* ninja warrior fights. A few flicks of my blades and she'd be begging for mercy."

In the shadows, Stealth Elf's muscles go tight. That's

it, she's heard enough. She slides her daggers silently from their sheaths. It's time to show these fakes what a *real* Skylander can do.

Should Stealth Elf take on all four of the evil minions? **Slice right over to page 34** if you think she should.

Or do you think she ought to keep hiding and listening out for more information? **Page 77 is where you want to be** if so.

Page 28

On the very rare occasions when Skylanders don't know what to do, they turn to their Portal Master. You've heard Hugo say that it's so much better to be safe than sorry, and this is one occasion where you think that's good advice. You decide the team should take some time to train before rushing off to investigate. Master Eon's big floating face doesn't look happy, but then he's not in charge of this particular adventure – you are.

"Great," says Cali. "I think you've made the right choice." She looks at the assembled Skylanders and smiles. "Now drop and give me fifty push-ups."

"Hey, you said we were doing a Heroic Challenge," complains Terrafin.

"Oh, don't worry – you will be," Cali replies. "But first I need you to get warmed up. Fifty push-ups, then three laps round the Ruins. Last one to finish has to listen to one of Flynn's stories."

"Did someone say 'story'?" asks Flynn. "Well, there was this one time . . ."

The Skylanders throw themselves to the ground and start doing push-ups as fast as they possibly can. None of them wants to be the last one back. Flynn's tall tales have been known to last for hours! Legend has it that Boomer once packed sticks of lit dynamite into his own ears just so he could avoid listening to a particularly long and rambling anecdote.

Terrafin finishes the push-ups first and springs to his feet. He sets off running, his stumpy legs powering him across the grass. There is a yelp of excitement from behind him and Hot Dog charges past, his tongue flapping happily in the wind.

"Get back here, ya flaming mutt!" Terrafin bellows loudly.

There's a great thundering of feet as the other Skylanders join in the race. Fright Rider streaks through the ranks on his powerful ostrich mount, Ozzy, overtaking Stealth Elf, and then Spyro. With a twitch of skeletal ostrich legs, Ozzy sprints right to the head of the pack, neck and neck with Hot Dog. They stay side by side the whole way round, neither one able to summon the energy for the final burst of speed that will push them into the lead.

Fright Rider and Hot Dog slide across the finish line at the same time. The other Skylanders all finish together just a few seconds later, panting and wheezing and out of breath.

"Who was last?" asks Flynn, who has already prepared a tale of high adventure.

"No one," smiles Cali. "They all came third. Good job, guys. Now, what's next? Do you want to go straight to the challenge, or try something a little more unpredictable first?"

If you think 'unpredictable' sounds like fun, **turn to page 48.**

If you'd rather send the Skylanders straight into the challenge, **turn to page 67.**

You head for the town on Shattered Island, and not a moment too soon! Buildings are burning all along the main street, and Mabu are running around, flapping their little arms in panic.

"Great, where's Gill Grunt when you need him?" Fright Rider sighs, as an elderly Mabu runs past with his beard on fire.

There is a *swish* of a blade and Stealth Elf slices the Mabu's beard clean off. The Mabu starts to smile with relief, then he spots Spyro and runs off in the opposite direction, screaming at the top of his voice.

"He's back! He's back! He's back to finish us off!"

"It wasn't me!" Spyro shouts after him, but his voice is drowned out by the crackling of the flames and the creaking of burning wood.

"Help, my babies!" shouts a Mabu woman. She is pointing up into a burning building, where you can just see the outline of two children clinging tightly together in the flickering flames.

"Got 'em!" barks Hot Dog, as he zips towards the building. Kicking with his hind paws he launches himself in through a downstairs window and is swallowed by the blaze.

Everyone holds their breath for what feels like forever, and then – *boom* – Hot Dog explodes through a hole in the wall upstairs, with the two Mabu children sitting on his back.

The Skylanders cheer and punch the air. "Great work, Bone Breath," cries Terrafin, but there's no time to celebrate properly.

"Everyone spread out," Spyro commands. "None of us has Water powers, so we're going to have to find some other way of stopping the fires."

Pop Fizz begins to hop from foot to foot. "Ooh, ooh!" he yelps, as he produces a test tube full of yellowish-green liquid. He turns and hurls it at the closest fire. There's a loud *whumpf* and the flames turn into something resembling marshmallow.

"Not bad at all," says Stealth Elf. "But do you have any more?"

With a grin, Pop Fizz turns, showing off his backpack. It is crammed with bottles, many of which are filled with the same yellowish-green liquid.

"Grab it all," Spyro tells the others. "Spread out, and let's get this fire under control!"

"Feel the motion of the potion!" Pop Fizz urges, as the Skylanders snatch the bottles from his bag and set about putting out the fires.

In no time the town is covered in gooey white marshmallow sludge. The fires have all been put out, but much of the town is ruined.

"Good work, everyone," says Spyro. "This could've been a whole lot worse if we hadn't got here in . . . Hey!"

A small rock bounces off Spyro's head with a *thud*.

You all turn to see an angry group of Mabu villagers approaching. Some of them carry sticks, while others are taking aim with rocks.

"You did this!" a Mabu near the front says. They're all staring at Spyro as they draw steadily closer. "You destroyed our homes."

"It wasn't me!" Spyro protests, but the Mabu don't seem to be in the mood to listen.

This is a delicate situation, Portal Master. It must be handled with the utmost care, or Spyro might end up getting whacked with sticks, and no one wants that. Especially Spyro.

Should Spyro try to convince the Mabu he wasn't responsible for the attack? If you think he's the best Skylander for the job, **turn to page 60**.

If you think the other Skylanders might have more luck talking sense into the Mabu, **negotiate your way to page 40**.

You're sick of hearing the impostors trash-talking. You're not going to stand in Stealth Elf's way. She steps out into sight. She is immediately spotted by the Evil Terrafin, but makes no move to retreat or attack. The shark minion's jaws snap shut. He and the other minions all close in on Stealth Elf. There is a faint *boing* as Evil Gill Grunt fires his harpoon. With a *thunk* the harpoon shoots straight through Stealth Elf's chest . . .

   . . . and a bundle of straw emerges from her back!

"It's a decoy!" yelps Evil Stealth Elf.

"Looks like you losers aren't the only duplicates," smirks the real Stealth Elf, appearing behind the villains.

Before they can turn and fight, she summons the magical Shadowsbane blades to aid her. They swish and slice at the enemies as Stealth Elf uses her acrobatic fighting skills to cut the duplicates down to size.

Surprise is on Stealth Elf's side. She defeats the minions before they can even get a single hit in.

As the last villain falls, they all crumble into dust. Stealth Elf slides her blades back into their sheaths. She taught them a lesson all right, but now you'll never find out what they were up to.

Yes, you may have won this battle, but I'm afraid it looks like you might just have lost the war.

THE END

You decide all this punching is getting you nowhere –
it's time for Terrafin to try one of his other attacks.

Before he can, the Arkeyan Hammah unleashes a
series of attacks of his own. Terrafin manages to deflect
the worst of the blows, but a few sneak through.

"You know you're just making me angrier, right?"
Terrafin snarls, as the Hammah's weapon sends him
spinning across the floor. Terrafin gets up and races at
the Hammah, but seems to slow as he reaches the robot,
giving it time to swing upwards with its weapon.

You watch in horror as Terrafin is sent spiralling
backwards. The evil minions exchange high-fives,
believing the battle to be well and truly over.

Terrafin has other ideas. As he falls to the ground he
burrows down beneath the surface and tears towards
the Hammah, churning the earth around him in his wake.

With a bellowed war cry, Terrafin explodes from
under the ground by the Hammah's feet. The robot
swings down sharply with his weapon, but Terrafin is
one step ahead. Twisting in the air he leaps, throwing
his arms out to the side. Bent forward, the weak spot in
the Hammah's force field is revealed. With a spectacular
belly flop, Terrafin destroys the shield and crashes down
on the robot's head.

Terrafin stands up to reveal a perfectly flat Arkeyan

Hammah squished against the ground where he landed.

"You . . . beat him," whimpers Evil Gill Grunt. "How? Kaos supercharged him up! He was unstoppable!"

"You call that *supercharged*?" Terrafin snorts. "Nothing's unstoppable. Except me."

"Way to go, Terrafin!" cheers Pop Fizz.

"Tell you what," grins Terrafin. "Since I got to take down tinhead, you take on these guys." He gestures to the evil minions, who glance nervously at one another.

"No way," says Spyro, as he and the other Skylanders step forward. "That's one battle we're not missing."

Terrafin shrugs. "Fair enough." He turns to the minions and bares his teeth. "Looks like we're all going to pound on you. This day just gets better and better!"

The evil doubles look at the Skylanders. Then they scream, turn, and run away as fast as they can.

The evil doubles of Chop Chop and Stealth Elf run off along a passageway on the right, while the fake Terrafin and Gill Grunt race down a corridor on the left. You still think it's important to keep the team together where possible, so who are you going to chase? Hurry, Portal Master, before they get away!

If you want to go after Chop Chop and Stealth Elf, **zoom to page 75**.

If you'd rather hunt down Terrafin and Gill Grunt, **get yourself over to page 23** right away.

You decide a good old-fashioned punch-up is the answer, and send the Skylanders charging after the evil doubles, despite Stealth Elf's protests.

Your team of heroes has barely made it up the first few steps before the minions make a run for it. As Spyro and the others give chase, something explodes on the stairs in front of them. A gang of Boom Fiends toss bombs down from the cliff top high above.

Caught off guard, the Skylanders can't defend themselves in time. A rain of explosives brings the steps crashing down around them, and as you watch the Skylanders tumble down into the darkness you wonder if perhaps you should have listened to Stealth Elf, after all.

THE END

You reckon just a few minutes of precious rest won't hurt anyone. I mean, it's not like a town full of poor innocent Mabu has just been attacked by someone who looks like Spyro or anything like that, is it?

Actually, hold on. That's exactly what has just happened, isn't it?

Master Eon's big floaty face appears. He looks even more unhappy than he did earlier. In fact, you can't remember Master Eon ever appearing to be this annoyed before.

"Just you take your time," Master Eon says, looking completely exasperated. "Lie there all day if you like. I have asked some of the other Skylanders to investigate the attack. Perhaps they'll take the situation a little more seriously than you have.

"And as for you, young Portal Master," he says, turning your way. "It seems that perhaps you are not as ready for the role as I first thought."

"Wait, Master Eon," says Spyro, but it's too late. As Master Eon fades from view, you and the Skylanders realize that you've made a very bad decision to rest at this crucial point. The other team are off saving the day and taking all the glory, and despite the glorious sunshine blazing overhead, your squad of Skylanders looks much more miserable than you have ever seen them before.

Still, this is Skylands, so a new danger – and a new adventure – is almost certainly just around the corner . . .

THE END

You decide it's safest to keep Spyro out of the way at least for now, and think there's probably a much better chance of the Mabu listening to one of the other Skylanders. The problem now is, which one of them should you pick?

Fright Rider? No, far too terrifying. Undead Skylanders can really give people the heebie jeebies on occasion.

Terrafin? No. Again, much too terrifying. He's a shark with arms and legs. Perhaps unsurprisingly, that doesn't tend to put many people at ease.

Pop Fizz? No, too . . . well, just too weird. Besides, he'd only turn them all into purple and orange toads or something odd like that by mistake.

That just leaves Stealth Elf and Hot Dog to choose between, then. You decide to let Hot Dog do all of the talking, because – let's face it – who could possibly resist such a cute wittle puppy dog?

"Hey stop, everyone," Hot Dog says, padding over to face the oncoming villagers. The woman whose children Hot Dog saved tells everyone to halt and listen carefully to what he has to say to them. You give yourself a big pat on the back for sending Hot Dog to try to reason with them.

"I know you think that Spyro attacked the town, but

you have to trust me, it wasn't really him," Hot Dog explains. "It was actually an evil double of him that was created by Kaos."

"It was definitely Spyro!" calls a voice from the crowd. "I saw him. He was spitting hot, nasty fireballs out here, there and everywhere. I nearly got one somewhere really nasty, I did."

"Think really hard about all this," urges Hot Dog. "Think hard about all the things Spyro has done for you in the past. Do you really think he'd want to do this to you and your town?"

There's a general mumbling from the crowd of Mabu. "Well, he did help me when I got my head stuck tight in a bucket that one time," admits a voice from near the back of the throng.

"And he helped me put up those shelves a few weeks back. Really good job he made, too."

"And he fought off that army of trolls who were trying to kill us all, too. Mustn't forget that."

"Oh no," agree the other townsfolk. "Mustn't forget that."

"And he wants to help you again now," Hot Dog says. "We all do. We want to catch who did this and find out why they attacked you."

"But we can't do that if you keep on hurling rocks at my head," says Spyro, jumping out from behind the scenes and joining Hot Dog in front of the crowd. There are some embarrassed coughs from within the ranks of the villagers, and slowly, one by one, they drop their weapons to the ground.

"Sorry, Spyro, we just thought –"

"I know. Don't worry about it. Kaos can be pretty tricky when he wants to be," Spyro says. "Now, if you'll please excuse us, we've got a crazy evil double of me to catch!"

Suddenly, from out of nowherem Hugo drops down with a scream and dangles on a rope in front of Spyro's face. Everyone looks up to see Flynn's balloon hovering above the wreckage of the town. Flynn waves cheerfully back.

"Told you you wouldn't hit the ground!" he shouts.

The rope snaps, and Hugo hits the ground with an ungraceful thump.

"Sorry," shouts Flynn. "I take that back."

Hugo scrambles back to his feet and adjusts his glasses. "Skylanders, Skylanders, more evil doubles have been sighted up on Dragon's Peak. I suspect they're probably up to no good."

"Aw, rats," says Terrafin. "Decision time again. Hey, Portal Master, what are we supposed to do now?"

Should the Skylanders pursue the evil dragon minion to Falling Forest? If you think they should, **start the chase on page 11**.

Should they head for Dragon's Peak to find out what the other doubles are up to instead? **Clamber over to page 73** if so.

You decide to live dangerously. Well, you decide that Pop Fizz should live dangerously, and drink the potion himself.

"Don't try this at home," he warns the others, before he glugs down the colourful liquid.

For a moment, nothing happens.

A few seconds later . . . nothing happens.

And then, all of a sudden . . . nothing happens.

"Aw, great," sighs Pop Fizz. He raises his fists, determined to fight until the end, but then . . .

BURP!

Pop Fizz lets out a loud belch and a plume of blue mist drifts out of his mouth. Deep down in his stomach, something rumbles and gurgles. "Now this is more like it!" he cries, as his body begins to mutate.

The Hammah steps back as the Skylander's arms grow until his knuckles scrape the floor. His body almost doubles in size. His wispy blue fur becomes thick, coarse hair, and his teeth become jagged fangs. Pop Fizz's huge, bloodshot, angry eyes turn and fix the Hammah.

"Hey, no fair!" whimpers the Gill Grunt double, staring up at Pop Fizz's hulking beast form.

"Who said anything about it being fair?" grins Spyro. "Now you're going to see why you should never mess with the Skylanders!"

The Hammah swings and connects with his weapon, but the mutated Pop Fizz barely notices. He lunges for the Arkeyan machine, but the Hammah dodges and brings his weapon down on Pop Fizz's bare foot.

Pop Fizz lets out a roar so loud it shakes the walls of the cavern.

"Now you've just gone and made him mad," says Terrafin with a toothy grin.

Still roaring with rage, the beast-form Pop Fizz makes a charge for the Arkeyan Hammah. The evil doubles part to let the Hammah through as he retreats. The ground vibrates with each thundering footstep as Pop Fizz charges behind, head lowered, eyes ablaze and . . .

THONK!

The Hammah leaps out of harm's way at the last moment, and Pop Fizz charges head-first into the wall. You and the other Skylanders watch in horror as the mutated hero stumbles backwards clutching his skull.

A cheer rises up from the evil minions as Pop Fizz sinks to his knees, still holding his head. He begins to shrink. The potion is already wearing off. Poor Pop Fizz is going to be no match for the Arkeyan Hammah now.

Besides, he can feel a bad headache coming on. This is one Skylander who *really* needs to rest. Too bad, Portal Master. For a minute there it looked almost like you were going to make it.

THE END

45

You decide to let Terrafin's fists do the talking. A wise move, Portal Master. As you know, Earth Skylanders are powerful against the Tech Element. You did know that, right? It wasn't just a lucky guess?

Whatever the reason, Terrafin looks like a good choice. "It's feeding time!" he cries, charging for the Hammah and raining punches down on him. The force of each blow is staggering.

"Ha! See what happens when you mess with the Skylanders?" shouts Terrafin. He turns away from the Hammah and raises his hands in victory. The other Skylanders shoot him a worried look.

"You might want to look behind you," suggests Spyro.

Terrafin turns to find the Hammah glaring at him, completely unhurt by his attack.

"Didn't we mention his force field?" sniggers Evil Gill Grunt. "Silly us."

The Hammah's weapon slams into Terrafin, sending him hurtling across the cavern. He hits the wall. For a moment you think the battle may be over.

But then a grin creeps across Terrafin's face, revealing his razor-sharp teeth. "So, you want to play rough?" he asks, slipping on his brass knuckles.

With a roar, Terrafin cuts loose with a furious attack. His fists fly, the brass knuckles pounding like sledgehammers against the Hammah's shield. The might of each blow is enough to make the force field tremble.

"Come on you ugly hunk of junk, fight!" snarls Evil Stealth Elf.

"Hey, who are you calling ugly?" cries the Chop Chop duplicate. "It looks exactly like me!"

"My point exactly," sneers the evil elf minion.

Terrafin delivers a right hook, then a flurry of powerful jabs. The robot's force field flickers with each punch. One final big punch and it should all be –

WHAM!

The robot's weapon swings up. It connects hard with Terrafin's chin, sending the Skylander into a backwards flip. He lands on the ground, face-down, not moving. You stare on in disbelief. How could he have lost?

"You know," growls Terrafin, getting back to his feet. "That almost hurt."

You and the other Skylanders let out a sigh of relief. Terrafin's definitely not out of the fight yet!

He raises his fists for battle again. You wonder if his punches are going to be enough. He may need another plan of attack.

If you think Terrafin should continue trying to punch the Hammah into submission, **turn to page 16**.

Or, if you think the time has come to try something else, **head quickly to page 35**.

You think it's good to keep the Skylanders on their toes, so you decide to give them 'something a little more unpredictable' to do.

Unfortunately, that 'something unpredictable' turns out to be Boomer, the dynamite-loving troll. At Cali's signal, he comes trudging up the hill carrying the largest stick of dynamite you or the Skylanders have ever seen.

Boomer stops at the top of the hill and grins at his fellow Skylanders. "I've brought the boom," he announces, and the others exchange worried glances.

"Boomer has invented a training game," Cali explains. "What's it called again, Boomer?"

"Catchy Catchy Boom Boom!"

"It's called Catchy Catchy Boom Boom," Cali says. She takes a few steps backwards and you realize that Flynn is hiding in the basket of his balloon, his hands held over his head. "Ready?" asks Cali, and before the Skylanders can reply she shouts, "Go!"

"Catchy Catchy," yells Boomer. He lights the stick of dynamite and hurls it towards Spyro, who swats it with his tail, sending it flying in Stealth Elf's direction.

Stealth Elf's ninja instincts take over. She launches the dynamite towards Fright Rider with a spinning kick. A quick flick from Fright Rider's jousting spear sends the explosive tumbling towards Pop Fizz.

Pop Fizz catches the dynamite. He gives it a sniff.

"Boom Boom!" laughs Boomer, and an explosion rocks the Ruins. The blast is heard for miles around, and while it isn't strong enough to do the Skylanders any real harm, the force of the explosion means they have to rest.

Sorry, Portal Master, but your adventure is over before it has even begun.

THE END

You suspect sending all the Skylanders to one spot might be reckless, and decide to make things hard on the big baldy by giving him lots of targets to deal with.

The team spreads out and circles Kaos.

"Stay still you fools!" he bellows.

Hot Dog spits a ball of flame at one of Kaos' legs.

"Ouch!" Kaos hisses. He turns and swipes at the little Fire pup. As he does, Terrafin vaults over Fright Rider's back and uppercuts the tip of Kaos' nose.

"Ow, by dose!" yelps the villain. He straightens up in time to see Spyro coming towards him, fire billowing from his throat. The flames lick at Kaos' shiny head and he lets out a shriek.

"You're lucky I don't have hair!" Kaos cries. Before he can retaliate, Stealth Elf stabs her blades into his big toe.

Kaos wails. "What did I ever do to you?"

"Uh," says Hot Dog. "Attack Skylands, destroy the Core of Light, threaten everyone we know . . . ?"

"OK, but apart from *that*?" asks Kaos, slamming his foot down hard. Hot Dog leaps to safety just in time.

A crack zigzags across the floor from Kaos' foot. The Skylanders jump clear, then watch as the crack snakes over to the rock Glumshanks is hiding behind. The rock splits to reveal the troll at the controls of a machine. You and Spyro recognize it at the same time.

"How did you get the Dragon's Throne?" asks Spyro.

"By defeating the Dragon King!" boasts Kaos.

"No you didn't," says Glumshanks. "We stole it when he wasn't looking. You cried when we thought we heard him coming back, remember?"

"Shut up," hisses Kaos, flicking Glumshanks away with one finger. "Even that idiotic Dragon King didn't realize the power the throne has. Thanks to my genius I've harnessed that power, and now I'm UNSTOPPABLE!"

With the tip of a finger he flicks a lever on the device. The Dragon's Throne pulses red and the floor beneath it trembles with earthquake force. A blast of concentrated magical energy hits Kaos and he grows up and out, until his head scrapes against the ceiling. The energy crackles behind his eyes, making them glow like two bright suns.

"Fear Ultra-Kaos!" he booms.

Terrafin cups his hands around his mouth and shouts, "Don't make me come up there and beat you, Kaos!"

You doubt a few punches from Terrafin is going to be enough to take this enormous Kaos down. Luckily, being the wise Portal Master that you are, you might just have one last trick up your sleeve . . .

If you want the Skylanders to unleash the full force of their might on Ultra-Kaos, **turn to page 71**.

If you want to reveal that one last trick I mentioned, **turn to page 59**.

"The exit is right around this next corner," says Fright Rider. "I'm sure of it."

"How sure?" sighs Spyro.

"Really sure. Couldn't be more sure."

"You said that two hours ago," groans Stealth Elf. "Right before we were attacked by those Stump Demons."

"But man, it was fun pummelling those guys," Terrafin says. "I don't think I'll ever get tired of punching evil trees in the face."

"Good times," agrees Hot Dog.

"But we've been bumbling along in the dark ever since," Spyro says.

"Speak for yourself," snorts Stealth Elf. "I don't *bumble*, I *slink*."

"Listen to me, guys," says Fright Rider. "We're not far away. Just around this corner. I'm absolutely sure."

The Skylanders trudge around the corner and find . . . nothing at all. A brick wall blocks their path. It is impossible to go any further.

"OK, so maybe not *absolutely* sure," admits Fright Rider. He gives the wall a tap with his spear, hoping that it's fake. It isn't. The wall is rock solid.

There is a piece of paper neatly folded and stuck in a gap between two bricks. Pop Fizz plucks it free and unfolds it. Everyone recognizes Cali's handwriting.

"Whoops," Pop Fizz reads. "Looks like you went the wrong way."

"Told you!" cries Hot Dog. "This nose is never wrong."

Pop Fizz turns the note over to see if there is anything else written on the back. When he sees that there isn't, he folds the note neatly again, then sticks it in his mouth and swallows it whole.

The other Skylanders all glare at Fright Rider. "Hey, don't blame me," says Fright Rider, pointing down at Ozzy. "Blame the ostrich!"

"Can you lead us out, Hot Dog?" asks Spyro.

The Fire pooch sniffs the air, then shakes his head. "I can't follow the path we took to get here. We've criss-crossed over our tracks too many times."

"Great," growls Terrafin. "Looks like we got a long night of walking ahead of us. I just hope we meet some more of them Stump Demons along the way."

THE END

"Let's get going," urges Spyro. "We need to find out what's happening and put a stop to it!"

Hugo clears his throat. "They, uh, they say it was you who attacked the town, Spyro," he says.

"We know that too, Hugo," Stealth Elf replies. "But it wasn't Spyro."

"Of course not," agrees Hugo. "But the Mabu are convinced it was. I suspect an evil minion double is responsible, and that means only one thing . . ."

"Kaos," growls Hot Dog.

"Of course," snaps Terrafin, punching his palm. "When I get my hands on that bald-headed little weirdo I'm going to pound him into the ground."

"You'll have to join the queue," says Fright Rider.

"I hear the town is in bad shape," Hugo continues. "The Mabu could use some help."

Spyro nods. "Then let's get going, there's no time to lose."

"On the other hand," says Hugo, "the evil double has been spotted in Falling Forest. There's no saying what he might be up to there."

"Uh-oh," groans Pop Fizz. "I feel another decision coming on."

"We could split up," suggests Stealth Elf. "Some of us go save the town . . ."

". . . And I'll go polish my knuckles on evil Spyro's head," nods Terrafin. "Good plan!"

But you're not so sure. You suspect that Kaos wants the team to split up, knowing they'll be weaker that way. You decide everyone should stick together. With Kaos up to his old tricks, it's going to take teamwork to win the day.

That still leaves you with a dilemma, though. Should you send the Skylanders to help the Mabu, or would you rather hunt down the nasty piece of work who caused all the problems in the first place? It's a tough call, but then no one ever said being a Portal Master was easy.

Well, except Flynn, but then he thinks Chompies are a type of fruit, so he isn't the best person to ask about anything.

To head to Shattered Island and help the Mabu, **turn to page 31**.

If you want to go to Falling Forest instead and kick some evil minion butt, **scoot over to page 22**.

Ooo-kay. So you've decided to pit a Magic Skylander against Tech opponent? Fair enough. You're the boss.

The Skylanders and the minions form a circle around Pop Fizz and the Arkeyan Hammah – heroes on one side, villains on the other. You and the Skylanders cheer as Pop Fizz races up and aims a powerful kick at the Hammah's chest, but the Arkeyan machine is protected by a force field, and the kick bounces harmlessly off.

"Hey, no fair!" cries Fright Rider from the sidelines.

"Who said anything about it being fair?" sneers the Gill Grunt double.

The Hammah swings with his weapon. Pop Fizz only just manages to roll to safety in time. As he does, bottles clatter from his backpack and roll across the cavern floor.

The Hammah swings again and again, each one closer than the one before. Pop Fizz scrambles backwards across the stone floor as another blow comes *crashing* down towards him, shattering the rock beside his feet.

Pop Fizz grabs a handful of the rock dust and throws it in the Hammah's face, trying to blind it. The robot's force field shields it from harm, though, and it is all Pop Fizz can do to leap up on to his feet and back away.

"Ha! Finish the coward!" booms the Stealth Elf double.

"Grind him into gremlin mince," cackles Evil Gill Grunt.

Hot Dog leans over and whispers to Spyro. "Should

we help him?"

Spyro shakes his head. "It's a matter of honour," he says. "If we rush in to rescue him, Pop Fizz will never live it down. He can win this. He just has to believe in himself!"

"I'm going to die!" shrieks Pop Fizz, running in circles around the Hammah.

Hot Dog shakes his head sadly. "He's probably not going to win this."

"I knew I should've taken the challenge," Terrafin groans. "I'd have turned that thing to scrap by now, force field or no force field."

You think Terrafin may be right . . . but wait! What's this? Pop Fizz manages to snatch up one of the potion bottles and pops the cork. The problem is, in all the confusion he's lost track of what potion does what, and doesn't know if he should lob this at the Hammah or drink it himself.

This is Pop Fizz's moment of need, Portal Master. You must help him decide!

Should he hurl the potion at the Arkeyan fighting machine? If so, **launch yourself across to page 17**.

Or should he drink the contents himself in the hope that the potion grants him some sort of special ability? **Make a quick-change to page 44** if you think this is the best course of action.

I see you like the direct approach, Portal Master. You and Terrafin have a lot in common.

You tell the Skylanders to all charge at once. Kaos' massive left foot isn't too far away, so Spyro and the others lock their sights on it and start running towards it.

"Take him down!" cries Spyro, leading the dash. Fright Rider grips his spear. Stealth Elf readies her blades. One attack combining all their powers should be enough to bring Kaos down . . . you think.

Unfortunately, that turns out not to be the case. Kaos lifts his foot, and the Skylanders are plunged into darkness as the shoe's shadow passes over them. The heroes try to run, but it's no use. Kaos' foot hits the ground with a loud *splat*, and a muffled cry of "ouch!"

"See what happens when you misbehave?" hollers the enormous villain. "Daddy Kaos has to put his foot down! Glumshanks!"

"Yes, Lord Kaos?" says Glumshanks, popping out from behind his rock.

"Hop up here into my pocket," commands Kaos. "We've got a world to conquer!"

I'm sorry, Portal Master, but your team of Skylanders needs a rest. And probably major surgery. Until then, their adventure – and yours – is well and truly over.

THE END

You decide the time has come to play your Ace. Using the Portal of Power you summon a new ally to help out.

"Hail to the Whale!" booms Thumpback, the whale-like Water Giant.

The Skylanders *oooh* in surprise. Thumpback is much taller than them, but is still tiny compared to Ultra-Kaos.

He isn't about to let that stop him, though. Swinging his anchor, he sends it slamming into Kaos' kneecap. Thumpback and Kaos are locked in a heated battle.

With Kaos kept busy, the Skylanders examine the contraption around the Dragon's Throne.

"Maybe we can reverse it," Fright Rider suggests.

"Oh yeah? And how do we do that?" snaps Terrafin.

Stealth Elf points to a switch marked *REVERSE*. "That one, maybe?"

Spyro shrugs. "Looks good to me." He hits the button and a swirl of magical energy shoots out. Suddenly, Kaos begins to shrink – and fast.

"Nooooo!" he wails, as he returns to normal size.

You watch happily as Kaos sprints off, with Thumpback and the Skylanders in pursuit. You know the baddie won't get far, and that Skylands is safe once again. You have done well, Portal Master. Master Eon will be proud.

THE END

"Back up, guys," Spyro tells the other Skylanders. "It's me the Mabu have a problem with. At least, they *think* it's me they have a problem with."

"I don't know, Spyro," says Hot Dog. "They sure do look pretty mad. Maybe you should let one of us do the talking this time. Just look at them. They've got themselves worked up into such a state that they probably won't even listen to you."

"Me! Me!" cries Pop Fizz excitedly, but luckily Stealth Elf clamps a hand over his mouth before he has a chance to make matters even worse.

The Skylanders reluctantly follow Spyro's orders and step back, leaving their dragon friend to face the advancing army of angry Mabu alone. And boy, do they look angry!

"Our homes!" they cry out, waving their sticks aggresively and hefting their heavy stones from hand to hand. "You! You have completely destroyed our precious homes!"

"My poor little 'uns could've been badly hurt!" shouts the mother of the little children Hot Dog rescued. "You should be ashamed of yourself. It's lucky the Skylanders turned up to help us when they did!"

Spyro takes a big, nervous step back as the group closes in around him. "But I'm a Skylander too! You know that! I've helped you guys out of scrapes hundreds of times before. Don't you remember?"

A frying pan sails through the air and *clanks* down on the ground by Spyro's feet. Then a large stone whistles past just above his head, narrowly missing one of his horns. The Mabu folk don't win any beauty contests even at the best of times, but this crowd is starting to get seriously ugly.

"You're a traitor!" shouts out one elderly Mabu man on a wobbly walking stick.

"And a town wrecker!" adds another angry resident.

"And your toenails are way too long!" shouts a third. He blushes a bright shade of scarlet when everyone else in the crowd turns around to look at him. He quietly adds, "Well, they are a bit, aren't they?"

"They're claws, not toenails," says Spyro, a little offended. "And it was one of Kaos' minions who attacked the town, not me!"

Despite Spyro's very best efforts, the angry gathering of Mabu aren't listening. As far as they are concerned, there's only one dragon to blame, and that's Spyro. They move in to attack, and there's nothing the Skylanders can do but retreat. After all, the Mabu aren't bad, just confused. The Skylanders can't possibly fight back or use their weapons against these opponents.

As the Skylanders quickly fall back, you realize there's now absolutely no chance of getting any information from the Mabu about the attack. The evil minion double's trail will be cold by now, too, which means that this mission is well and truly over.

THE END

"Your Portal Master is right," says Master Eon, nodding his approval. "Training is very important, but not when there are others who may be in danger. For all we know, Spyro . . . I mean, *whoever it was who attacked the village* . . . is still there."

Just then, Hugo comes running up the hill as quickly as his little legs can carry him, puffing and panting loudly all the way. He staggers to a stop at the top of the hill and bends over, his hands resting on his knees as he fights to get his breath back. "Something . . . very . . . important . . . to tell . . . you," he wheezes.

"Well hurry up, then," snaps a deeply frustrated Terrafin. "We've actually got quite a big emergency happening here, you know?"

Hugo nods, causing his glasses to almost slide off his face, which is damp with sweat from all his running. He pushes them back up onto his nose as he struggles to catch his breath. "One . . . second," he pants. "Bear . . with . . . me."

The Skylanders stand around, impatiently tapping their feet and claws as they wait for Hugo to get his breathing back under control. Hot Dog passes the time by chasing his tail all over the place, and looks more than a little disappointed when he inevitably fails to catch up with it.

"Could we maybe hurry this up a little, Hugo?" asks Spyro.

Hugo nods again. "Yes," he pants. "Sorry. Almost . . . there."

A few more big breaths later and Hugo straightens up again. "There," he says. "That's better. I'm always surprised by how steep that hill is. I'm not as fit as I used to be."

"Hugo, old pal, you were never as fit as you used to be," says Flynn. "I, on the other hand, am as fit as I ever will be."

Cali looks a bit confused. "What's that supposed to mean, Flynn?"

"I honestly have no idea," admits Flynn.

"Can we please get on with it?" sighs Stealth Elf. "What's the something important you have to tell us all, Hugo?"

"Oh yes, I almost forgot about that," says Hugo. "A Mabu town has been attacked."

The Skylanders groan.

"On, um, Shattered Island."

"We know!" yelps Hot Dog. "That's where we were going before you arrived and made us wait all this time, while you puffed and panted."

Hugo blushes slightly. "Oh. Were you? Well . . . very good. Off you go, then."

Hugo steps aside and the Skylanders start to move

off. This time, though, it's Master Eon who stops them from heading on their way.

"Hold fast, Skylanders," he says. "I've been thinking . . . Training might not be a good idea, but perhaps it would be a wise idea for you to upgrade your abilities before charging off? As you know, Persephone is always happy to help in that regard."

You look over to the tree where the fairy's station is located. Persephone bobs gently up and down in the air, her blue wings fluttering lightly on the breeze. She seems to be holding a conversation with a tiny caterpillar that is busily crawling up and down one of her fingers. From the way she is laughing, it must be one seriously funny little bug.

"I'm always up for an upgrade," nods Hot Dog.

"Speak for yourself, bone breath," snorts Terrafin, as confident in his own abilities as ever. He cracks his knuckles and smiles. "Some of us are already at the top of our game."

Giving the Skylanders a bit of a power boost may not be such a bad idea. There's no saying what you might face out there.

Then again, those Mabu might be in danger. If you stop to upgrade you may not make it on time to help them.

So which is it to be, Portal Master?

If you want to pop round to Persephone's and level up
the Skylanders' abilities, **turn to page 9** right away.

If you think your little team are just perfect as they are,
head straight over to page 54.

You decide that 'something unpredictable' sounds dangerous. Besides, once training is finished you've got an attack to investigate. There's no time to muck around.

"OK, the Heroic Challenge it is," Cali says.

"Excellent choice," Flynn adds. "It reminds me of a decision I was forced to make one time. There I was, Chompies to the left of me, Spell Punks to the right, armed only with some cardboard and a broken pencil . . ."

"Quick, go!" says Cali. "Portal Master . . . send them to the dungeons."

In the blink of an eye you transport the Skylanders to the creepy Skylands dungeons now used by Cali as one of her many training grounds. The group appear in the heart of an underground maze, lit up by spooky flickering torches. Somewhere in the distance, something lets out a deep, rumbling roar.

"Well isn't this nice?" says Spyro.

"Who do I gotta punch to get outta here?" asks Terrafin.

"I think it's a maze," says Fright Rider.

"Then let's find the way out," suggests Stealth Elf.

There are two exits leading out of the room in opposite directions. Before anyone can choose which way to go, though, Hot Dog lets out a low growl. "I smell trouble," he says.

His warning comes just in the nick of time. A split second later, the room is filled with dozens of Haunted Knights. They clank closer and closer to the Skylanders, waggling their swords, their dark armour gleaming in the torchlight.

"There must be sixty of them," Spyro says.

"And only six of us," adds Stealth Elf. "Or seven, if you count Fright Rider twice."

"Not fair, not fair," says Pop Fizz.

Terrafin smiles, revealing his sharp teeth. "You're right. Maybe we should tie our hands behind our backs so they at least have a chance."

The Skylanders think about this for a moment. "Nah!" they laugh, and then they leap into action. Fireballs fly, blades clash, and knuckle dusters crunch against armour.

With a swig of a potion, Pop Fizz transforms into a monstrous blue creature. He barrels through a squadron of knights, knocking them over like skittles. In no time at all, every one of the Haunted Knights lies in a crumpled heap on the cold stone floor.

"They didn't stand a *ghost* of a chance," says Spyro. He smiles at the others. "Get it? Ghost?"

"We get it," sighs Stealth Elf, as she silently puts her daggers away. She looks at the two doors in turn. "The question is, which route do we take?"

"This way," says Fright Rider, pointing to the left hand door. "Ozzy's Undead senses say this door leads us to the exit."

"My nose says differently," argues Hot Dog. He sniffs the floor by the right hand door. "I smell fresh air this way. This is the door we should go through."

"This one," insists Fright Rider.

"This one!" insists Hot Dog.

"There's only one way to settle this," says Spyro. "Let's ask the Portal Master!"

So what's it to be, oh wise and wonderful Portal Master?

If you think everyone should follow Fright Rider's lead, **turn to page 52.**

If you'd prefer to trust Hot Dog's nose, **head on over to page 18.**

Lowering his horned head, Spyro charges straight for the evil double hiding in the undergrowth.

With a roar of triumph he crashes into the clump of bushes, only to find the evil minion has jumped out of harm's way! Spyro suddenly realizes there is no ground beneath his feet. He has charged right over the edge of a cliff!

As he plunges towards the ground, Spyro tries to open his wings, but more vines have become tangled around them, pinning them to his back. He struggles against the vines, but it's no use. They're too tight for him to break, and he can't turn his head far enough to burn them off.

Over the whistling of the wind, Spyro can hear the laughter of his evil double. The distant ground races up. Spyro lets out a groan. He's had his fair share of crash landings in his time, but he has a horrible feeling that this one will be the worst of them all.

THE END

So . . . what? You're sending the teeny tiny Skylanders to face Ultra-Kaos all by themselves? Were those hints about the trick up your sleeve not strong enough or something? Oh dear.

The Skylanders band together for one final attack, even though they clearly don't think it's a very good idea. You can see it in their eyes. They know they're doomed, but they believe their Portal Master must have a cunning plan.

Sadly, they're wrong.

Despite their best efforts, Kaos barely even notices their attack. With a single punch he explodes out of the cavern and up onto Dragon's Peak.

"So long, Sky-*losers*," he bellows, and with a twitch of his legs he leaps over to the next island. The Skylanders can only listen helplessly as he sets about destroying everything and everyone in sight.

The era of Skylanders and Portal Masters is over. The reign of Kaos, on the other hand, has begun!

THE END

You decide to put Spyro's fireball attack to work. I mean, what could possibly go wrong with that plan . . .?

On your command, Spyro opens his mouth and spews fire into the dark recess ahead of him. The flames burn blindingly hot, and in a matter of moments all that remains of the evil Chop Chop double is a charred helmet and a smoking pair of shoes.

Great! Hooray! Three cheers! Thanks to you, Spyro has turned that wicked minion to dust! He won't be bothering anyone again in a hurry!

Of course . . . the Skylanders are still completely and utterly stuck, and the whole place is about to shake itself to bits, but hey, at least that pesky Chop Chop impostor has been taken care of, right?

I don't know, Portal Master, sometimes I wonder if you're even trying.

As the earth tremor starts to bring the walls and ceiling down around the Skylanders' ears, you notice the Stealth Elf clone slipping away to safety. You wish you knew where she was going and what Kaos was up to, but now you'll never know, as a thousand tonnes of rubble come crashing down on your team, trapping them there in the dark for a long, long time to come.

THE END

You reckon a group of evil doubles sounds more dangerous than one evil double on its own, so send the Skylanders to Dragon's Peak to investigate.

The team finds itself standing at the top of a stone staircase. Spyro leads the way down to the bottom, and the Skylanders step onto a grassy clearing at the foot of a high cliff. The clearing is filled with large, strange-looking plants. Something about the plants looks very familiar. It takes a few seconds for Stealth Elf to remember where she's seen them before.

"Chompy Pods!" she cries, just as the plants all burst open, spitting Chompies in all directions.

The Skylanders leap into action. Hot Dog lets rip with his Firebark and several Chompies go up in smoke. Terrafin, Fright Rider and Pop Fizz charge for the others, punching and jabbing and kicking at them.

Meanwhile, Spyro and Stealth Elf take care of the pods. As Spyro burns through half of them, Stealth Elf carves up the others with her blades. In no time at all the clearing is a Chompy-free zone.

"Woo-hoo!" cries Pop Fizz, but Hot Dog stops him before he can say any more.

"Ssh," Hot Dog urges. His ears twitch as he listens to something the others can't hear. "Voices. This way."

He pads quietly over to the cliff wall and peeks

around the corner. There, walking up some steps are four more of Kaos' minions. All four of them look almost exactly like one of the Skylanders. There are doubles of Stealth Elf, Chop Chop, Gill Grunt and Slam Bam. They are talking as they make their way up the steps, but they are too far away for even Hot Dog's ears to make out what they're saying.

"Should we attack?" asks Terrafin. "We should attack, right? I think we should attack."

"Then we may not find out what they're up to," Stealth Elf replies.

"I could beat it out of them," Terrafin suggests. "That wouldn't be a problem. Really. I'd be happy to."

"No," insists Stealth Elf. "I should follow them and listen in."

Once again, the decision is in your hands, Portal Master.

If you like Terrafin's plan of pummelling the bad guys until they reveal what they are up to, **battle your way to page 37**.

If you think Stealth Elf should use her impressive ninja skills to follow the villains and discover their plan, **creep on over to page 25**.

You send the Skylanders down the right hand corridor, after Evil Chop Chop and Evil Stealth Elf. The passage is dark, and the team has to move in single file. The corridor narrows and the Skylanders have to squeeze through, the walls pressing against them on either side.

"Well, this is comfortable," groans Fright Rider sarcastically. Ozzy, his Undead skeletal ostrich, pads along behind him, not bothered by the size of the gap. That's one of the advantages of being a living skeleton.

"I'm getting a little stuck here," Spyro warns from the front. His wings are folded up against his back and his shoulders are wedged against the rough stone walls. The gap ahead of him is narrower still, but he can just make out something moving in the shadows.

There is a yelp of surprise from the back of the line, as something slams hard against Pop Fizz's back. You are just able to catch a glimpse of the evil Stealth Elf double before she melts away into the darkness again.

"I've got a bad feeling about this," Terrafin mutters.

"Move back, Pop Fizz," urges Stealth Elf.

"I can't!" Pop Fizz says. The kick from the minion has wedged him between the walls. He can't wriggle free.

"Here, let me help," says Terrafin. He shoves hard, using his rounded shoulder to try to push Pop Fizz free.

"Ouch!" yelps the gremlin, and for a moment it looks

like his eyes are going to pop out. Then Terrafin stops pushing and Pop Fizz's eyes return to their normal size.

Spyro peers into the darkness ahead. The shape he saw draws closer and he realizes it is the Chop Chop double. The evil minion's skeletal frame is thin enough to fit. Wedged in tight, Spyro can only watch as the minion approaches, his sword raised and ready to attack.

With both ends of the line stuck, the Skylanders are at the mercy of two villains. Can things get any worse?

Almost immediately, things get worse.

The walls begin to tremble and shake, as if the whole of Dragon's Peak is caught in an earthquake. Small rocks and lumps of stone shake loose from the ceiling and *ping* off the Skylanders' heads. The vibrations of the walls rattle their teeth, and the knock-knock-knocking of Ozzy's bones are deafening in the cramped space.

Oh dear, Portal Master, things are looking grim for your Skylanders. It's decision time again, so choose wisely – your team's lives may very well depend on it.

Just don't take long, or you'll be looking at the world's most heroic pancakes . . .

If you think Spyro should fireball blast the evil Chop Chop, **turn to page 72**.

On the other hand, if you think Pop Fizz should take a swig of a potion and hope for the best, **get yourself over to page 14**.

While there's little you'd enjoy more than seeing Stealth Elf do a number on the evil doubles, you decide it's more important to discover the bigger picture.

As the minions head through one of the many doors, Stealth Elf slips through with them. They carry on boasting about how tough they are as they stomp along a corridor and into a wide cavern.

"So we just gotta wait here?" asks Evil Terrafin.

"That's what Kaos says," replies the wicked Stealth Elf double.

"And Kaos knows best!" chirps Evil Chop Chop. The other doubles shoot him another look. "Well . . . OK, he doesn't *actually* know best, obviously."

"What's his plan this time?" sighs Evil Gill Grunt. "Killer fruit? Exploding trousers?"

"Guess we just hang around here until we find out," shrugs Terrafin's duplicate, and he sits on the floor of the cavern to wait.

This looks just like the perfect time to go back for the other Skylanders. Stealth Elf tiptoes quietly back the way she came, only to find Spyro and the others standing in the hallway trying to make a decision on which door to head through.

"What are you all doing here?" she asks.

"We got bored waiting, so we came to look for you,"

Hot Dog explains.

"Speak for yourself," says Terrafin. "I'd just found a whole gang of Boom Fiends to pound on. I was having the time of my life."

"Quiet or they'll hear us," Stealth Elf warns. She explains that the minions are waiting in the cavern for Kaos to arrive. Then she leads the Skylanders stealthily along the corridor. As they near the end, two of the bottles in Pop Fizz's backpack *clink* together noisily.

The Skylanders suddenly all freeze, expecting to hear shouts or alarm bells at any moment. But there is no sound from the opening ahead of them.

Pop Fizz flashes a nervous, apologetic smile, then follows the others as they continue along the passageway.

As one, they poke their heads around the corner, only to find the cavern empty! The minions have vanished – or so you think . . .

"See, told you I heard something," snaps the Terrafin duplicate.

"Hey, that's one good looking guy," grins the real dirt shark. Then his expression turns serious and he cracks his knuckles together. "Shame I'm gonna have to rearrange that pretty face."

"Hold up there, tough guy," says Evil Gill Grunt, holding up his hands. "What's say we settle this with a duel? One of you against one of us."

"Or we could all just attack you at once," says Spyro.

"You could," admits the Stealth Elf duplicate. "If you're too afraid to accept the challenge."

Terrafin and Pop Fizz both step forward. "Challenge accepted," they both say at the same time.

"I'm doing it," growls Terrafin.

"Me, me!" yelps Pop Fizz.

"Maybe this will help make up your minds," says the Chop Chop double with a smirk. "Allow me to introduce your opponent."

"You said it was one of you," Spyro reminds him.

"Yes," sniggers the minion. "But I lied. Although . . . he does look a bit like me."

There is a loud clanking and whirring from the corner of the cavern. A robotic figure marches straight towards the gathered Skylanders. In its hands it carries something that looks part hammer, part spear, and *all* deadly.

You recognize the ancient armour at once – it is an Arkeyan Hammah! Its red eyes burn like hot coals as it closes in on the heroes. Pop Fizz and Terrafin don't seem worried, though, and are still arguing over who gets to fight it.

Remember, Portal Master, this enemy is strong with the power of the Tech Element, so which Skylander do you think is best suited to the battle?

If you think Terrafin should fight the Arkeyan Hammah, **turn to page 46**.

If you'd rather give Pop Fizz a chance to show what he can do, **turn to page 56**.